Deaf Like Pluto

PRAISE FOR *STORYSHARES*

"One of the brightest innovators and game-changers in the education industry."
– Forbes

"Your success in applying research-validated practices to promote literacy serves as a valuable model for other organizations seeking to create evidence-based literacy programs."
- Library of Congress

"We need powerful social and educational innovation, and Storyshares is breaking new ground. The organization addresses critical problems facing our students and teachers. I am excited about the strategies it brings to the collective work of making sure every student has an equal chance in life."
– Teach For America

"Around the world, this is one of the up-and-coming trailblazers changing the landscape of literacy and education."
- International Literacy Association

"It's the perfect idea. There's really nothing like this. I mean wow, this will be a wonderful experience for young people."   - Andrea Davis Pinkney, Executive Director, Scholastic

"Reading for meaning opens opportunities for a lifetime of learning. Providing emerging readers with engaging texts that are designed to offer both challenges and support for each individual will improve their lives for years to come. Storyshares is a wonderful start."
- David Rose, Co-founder of CAST & UDL

Deaf Like Pluto

Maya Bhattiprolu

STORYSHARES

Story Share, Inc.
New York. Boston. Philadelphia

Copyright © 2022 Maya Bhattiprolu

All rights reserved.

Published in the United States by Story Share, Inc.

The characters and events in this book are fictitious. Any similarity to real persons, living or dead, is entirely coincidental.

Storyshares
Story Share, Inc.
24 N. Bryn Mawr Avenue #340
Bryn Mawr, PA 19010-3304
www.storyshares.org

Inspiring reading with a new kind of book.

Interest Level: Middle School
Grade Level Equivalent: 3.5

9781642615326

Book design by Storyshares

Printed in the United States of America

Storyshares Presents

1

Space is completely silent to the human ear. Sounds do exist, "but in the form of electromagnetic vibrations that pulsate in similar wavelengths."

–canyouactually.com

My little brother is shaking me. *Wake up, Kaira,* he says. *You're going to be late.*

It wouldn't be the first time. My dad always calls us down, but I never hear him.

I quickly slip into my favorite pair of jeans and a random t-shirt I find in my drawer. When I get downstairs, Dad has already set a bowl of cereal on the table for me. He asks me if I slept well. I nod. The clock reads 7:22; three minutes before the bus comes.

I swallow the last of the milk in the bowl and sign *goodbye* to Dad. I make it out of the house just as the bus arrives.

How are you? the bus driver asks me as I climb into the bus. I sign the word "good" and sit behind him.

The seats are mostly empty. This bus is only for special needs kids or kids with disabilities. It's for the kids with Autism, the kids in wheelchairs, or the kids who are deaf and can't talk. Like me. I stare out the window, catching my reflection.

Callie, my older sister, once told me I'm pretty. I think she was trying to make me feel better because I'm deaf. I don't think I am pretty. I also have heterochromia, which makes my eyes two different colors. One of them is brown, and the other is hazel. Callie, on the other hand, has two green eyes. We both share the same hair color. But my hair is curly and frizzy while her hair is wavy and smooth.

Not being able to hear or speak is horrible. I would trade all of this to be in Callie's position. To be able to hear sounds. Sometimes it feels like I'm living in outer space, where I can't hear a thing. It can be cool, but sometimes I would rather be down on Earth.

The bus pulls up into the school's parking lot. *Thank you,* I sign to the bus driver. *You're welcome*, he replies.

I walk through the front doors and head to the principal's office. As I do so, I notice the kids in the hall staring at me. It's no different from any other day, but their eyes bore into my back. I can see them whispering to one another. I bet that I am the subject of their conversation.

One of them is a girl named Ginger. Her golden locks are styled in supple curls. She's been tormenting me since sixth grade (more than two years) because I'm deaf. I found a note in my locker last year. It said, "*Your dumb and your a deaf ugly person,*" the derogatory words being dumb (as in stupid and mute), and ugly. And I guess deaf was also meant to be derogatory. I just crumpled the note and threw it away. (Besides, why should I pay any attention to someone who can't even spell right?)

As I walk by, Ginger puts an L to her head and brings it forward, the sign for loser. Her friend, Grace, does the same.

They both laugh. I duck my head and keep walking.

It hasn't always been this way. I went to deaf school until third grade and then my dad homeschooled me. But he got a job at the end of fifth grade, so I was forced to go to public school. Unfortunately.

When I reach the front desk lady, a sweet, red-faced, woman, I sign hello and head into the principal's office.

2

Pluto's atmosphere is cooler and more compacted than scientists expected.

—space.com

A girl is sitting in my chair. She is talking to the principal.

As I walk in, they both look up.

Good morning, the principal mouths. She takes a piece of paper and a pen and writes something down. She holds it up.

Take a seat, it says. I do. Dr. Tumuaki scribbles a few more words. *This is Autumn. She's new here, and she would like you to show her around.*

I glance at her. She's got strawberry blonde hair, striking blue eyes, and pink lips. Bracelets are lined up her arm, and she's wearing a mustard yellow shirt with overalls. If I had to describe her in one word based on this first impression, I would say artistic. If I could speak.

She notices me staring at her. *Hello, my name is Kaira. Nice to meet you,* I quickly sign.

Hello, she signs.

I gape at her. *You know sign language?* I ask her.

She nods. *A little. Help me, please?*

Okay.

I show her the lockers first. The other kids, including Ginger and Grace, are still there. They watch as we walk past them. At first, I don't know who they are staring at, but then I realize they are staring at both of us.

We've already established that Ginger and Grace hate me. Most of the other kids do too. I'm the only deaf person in our grade. And I don't have any friends, so I guess it is surprising to see me walking with another girl.

My locker is near my science class, as is Autumn's. Our schedule is almost the same, except the period when she has language. During that time, I have a free period to work with my teachers.

Your locker, I sign, and then point to the locker. She looks confused. I repeat the sign, but she doesn't understand.

L, O, C, K, E, R, I spell out.

Her eyes widen. *I understand. Thank you.*

Autumn enters her locker combination. She jiggles the locker handle a bit and it pops out. Unzipping her backpack, she pulls out a blue-green ombre binder, a white notebook, and a pencil pouch.

I point to the binder. *Cool.*

Thank you, she replies. *I made it myself.*

Autumn stuffs the empty backpack into her locker and slams the door shut.

Ginger is standing there, and Grace is right beside her.

Hi, I'm Ginger. She speaks it, but I look at her lips to read what she is saying.

Autumn says something, and they go on talking for a while. Ginger occasionally flips her hair. Autumn plays with her bracelets. Grace and I just stand there.

Finally, I see the kids disperse, which means the bell rang. Ginger waves at Autumn and walks into the science lab.

Autumn smiles at me. I lead her into class. Bree, my aide, is standing next to the teacher's desk. She grins at me.

How are you? she asks.

Good, thank you. I point to Autumn. *She is Autumn. She is new.*

They chat until the teacher walks in. Bree and I walk to my seat. Autumn follows.

The science lab has counters instead of tables. Four people can sit at one counter. I sit by myself since all the other counters are full (except Ginger and Grace's), and Bree usually helps me with group assignments.

Autumn suddenly stops and turns around, so I look over. Ginger and Grace are there, probably asking her to sit with them. Autumn shakes her head and takes a seat next to me. I smile at her. Ginger narrows her piercing blue eyes at me and crosses her arms.

Bree taps me on the shoulder and starts signing what the teacher says. *We are moving on to a new topic,* Bree signs. *The solar system.*

Deaf Like Pluto

3

Pluto was reclassified as a dwarf planet in 2006 because it had not "cleared the neighborhood around its orbit."

–theplanets.org

    I love space, and everything in it. But what I really love about it are the planets. Pluto is my favorite, even though it isn't a planet anymore. Pluto and I are a lot alike. Pluto is...different. And it didn't fit in, so it was excluded. Kind of like me.

Bree taps me, and I focus on her hands.

Research a constellation. It's a group project, so find someone to work with.

I look at Autumn. *Partners?*

She smiles. *Yes.*

When lunch finally rolls around, I head to my locker to take out my lunchbox. I wait for Autumn to get out her lunch, but she just leans against the wall.

Where's your lunch?

I will buy, she responds. I grimace, and she laughs. *Bad?*

Yes!

We walk to the lunchroom. I normally eat lunch with Bree in the teacher's lounge, but I decided to accompany Autumn today.

Autumn stands in line and asks me what food is good.

Turkey sandwich, I say.

She picks one up, pays for it, and we look around for a seat.

Where do you sit? she asks me.

I'm about to respond when Autumn sees Ginger waving her over. She looks at me, and I shrug. We walk over to Ginger's table where Grace and the rest of Ginger's minions sit.

They all talk amongst themselves. I can't hear them, so I just sit and quietly eat my lunch. I can see Autumn talk sometimes, but mostly she and I sign with each other and make plans to work on our project. We decide on my house since she's still unpacking, but I warn her of my little brother.

At the end of lunch, we throw our trash away and go to our classes. Autumn has Spanish, so I show her the classroom and then head to the teacher's lounge to meet Bree.

Hello, Bree signs. *Good lunch?*

Yes, I respond. *I need help with English. Need to write an essay.*

Okay, she tells me. Bree gets a piece of paper and a pencil. *Let's start.*

4

Corona Borealis, the Northern Crown, is a myth where the jewels of the crown worn at Princess Ariadne's wedding turned into stars after being thrown into the sky.

-constellation-guide.com

Autumn and I meet up at the front of the school when class is finally over.

I must admit, I'm really excited. It's been a long time since I've had a friend over. The last time someone came over was in third grade, the year when I quit the deaf school. It's been almost five years!

Autumn smiles at me. *Ready?*

I nod. As we start walking, Ginger appears like an unexpected storm on a bright sunny day. Like an unwanted, embarrassing relative. Like a—well, you get the idea.

She smiles sweetly at Autumn, and they talk for a few seconds before Autumn hooks her arm through mine and leads me down the steps.

Oh my gosh, she signs. *I thought she would never leave.* Her lips turn up, and the corners of her mouth crinkle as she opens her mouth. I can tell she is laughing. I smile, and we sign all the way home.

I learn she has an older brother who's in college, she has a pet lizard, and she moved here because her parents got divorced. I tell her about Callie and Nick (my younger brother) and about my eyes.

I take my keys out when we reach my house. Callie has cross-country, so she stays late after school. Nick is still in elementary school, so he gets out later.

Wow, pretty, Autumn signs when she enters my house. I instruct her to take off her shoes, and we head upstairs to my room.

The walls are a cornflower blue, and the large windows light up the room. I have a solar system projector and a model hanging above my bed. My bed is in the center of the room and I have a giant teddy bear. There are posters of famous astronomers like Stephen Hawking and Neil deGrasse Tyson. My room also leads out to the balcony, and there are beanbag chairs, a small table, and a hammock that I added last year on my birthday.

This is so cool, she says when she sees it. *Let's work outside.*

I grab my computer, pieces of paper, and some markers. We step onto the balcony.

What should we research? Autumn asks.

I don't even have to think about it. *Corona Borealis.* It's my favorite constellation. My mom used to tell me about it, before she died, so I know all about the myth of Ariadne.

I pull up a webpage of facts about the constellation and point to it. Autumn blinks. *Wow, that was quick. Okay.*

I start to draw the constellation while she records the facts.

At one point, Nick comes to see what we are doing. I quickly push him out, but I see Autumn laughing so I already know he has told some embarrassing story about me. At five, her mom comes to pick her up. I hug Autumn.

Bye. See you tomorrow, I sign at the front door. She says bye and gets into the car.

5

2014 UZ224, a possible dwarf planet, was discovered on August 19, 2014, and considered a "friend" for Pluto.

-wikipedia.org

I wake up late the next day. It's Friday, the best day of the week. It's my favorite because it's when I take my art class. I'm also looking forward to seeing Autumn today. We're presenting our science project, so I stayed up late last night making it perfect. I decided to put it in a frame and add little lights to act as stars. It looks really cool, and I think Autumn will really like it. I hope.

I put on Callie's white, ripped Levi jeans (the rips are real) and an olive-green shirt (also Callie's). She sometimes lets me borrow her clothes, if she's in a good mood. And she is today since it's her birthday.

When I get downstairs, Callie gives me a hug and offers to drop me off at school since I missed the bus. I sign *yes* and wish her a happy birthday.

I grab the science project and my bag, and we get into the car. Callie drops me off at the main office.

Thank you, I tell her right before I get out. I have the frame in one hand. I go to the principal's office like I did yesterday.

Hi, the receptionist mouths. I wave back and enter Dr. Tumuaki's office. She is sitting at her desk talking to Autumn.

Autumn looks up when I walk in and smiles brightly.

Hello. She glances at the frame. *Cool! Is that our project?*

I nod. *I finished last night. Do you like it?*

Yes! It's so cool! She stands up. *The bell rang. Let's go.*

We rush to our lockers to put our bags away. We make it to science class with a minute to spare.

Ginger and Grace stare at us as we take our seat, but Autumn doesn't pay attention to them so neither do I. I continue to feel them glaring at us, but I shake it off and focus on Bree.

Who wants to go first? the teacher asks, and Bree translates.

Of course, Ginger and Grace volunteer. Without thinking, my hand goes up as well. I can tell the teacher is surprised because I never volunteer for anything and I usually go last.

She says something, and I look at Bree. *You can go next.*

Ginger and Grace saunter up to the front with a large poster of their constellation, Cassiopeia. I look at the section titled, "Why we chose this constellation." Underneath it, they wrote, "Because Cassiopeia was a queen and so are we."

I resist the urge to smile and break the truth to them: she was a mean queen. I have to say, it does fit pretty well.

When I see Autumn clapping, I assume they are done. I clap too. I look around the room and notice that the class looks bored and uninterested. Ginger curtsies. As she passes our table, she smirks at me and flips her hair, as if challenging me to do better.

Autumn stands up and pulls me with her. I grab the frame and hand her the notes to read. I turn on the lights on our project, and the other students' mouths drop.

Well, not really, but I can tell everyone else is amazed. Everyone but Ginger. Even Grace is paying attention. I glance at the science teacher and she is smiling at me. *Good job,* she mouths. I grin widely.

When we finish, I see everyone clapping. Even Ginger is clapping (a bit hesitantly, but still).

Autumn looks at me and smiles. *We did it,* she says.

A couple more people go and then the bell rings. I stay behind to talk with the teacher. Bree stays with me to translate. *I'm proud of you. That was really good.*

Thank you, I sign.

Keep up the good work. She smiles at me, and I take that as my cue to leave.

At the door, Autumn and another kid, Isaac, are waiting for me. He says something, and Autumn signs it for me.

That was so cool. You're smart.

Thanks, I sign. He smiles at me and walks off.

Autumn gives me a look, and I roll my eyes. She glances at my watch, and her eyes widen. *Let's go! We're going to be late!* She grabs my hand and pulls me to our next class.

* * *

At lunch, I don't want to sit with Ginger again and neither does Autumn. We sit at a table near the trash cans, the furthest one from Ginger. And yet, she still finds us.

She walks up to us with Grace and her other friends. She sneers at me and tries to engage in a conversation with Autumn, but Autumn doesn't pay any attention to Ginger.

I feel a kick on my leg. I look up.

They're making the Loser symbol at me again. I quickly duck my head and focus on my lunch. Autumn catches my eye and tells me to ignore them.

I feel another kick.

She's kicking me, I tell Autumn.

Her hands clench into fists and she stands up. I look at her lips. *Why can't you just leave us alone?* she says to Ginger. I can tell Ginger is taken aback because no one speaks to her like that.

I look at Ginger's lips. *Excuse me?*

I stand up. *You heard Autumn. Why are you so mean?* I sign this, and Autumn speaks it.

The other kids in the lunch room are now staring at us. I see Isaac come up behind Autumn.

Yeah, I see him say. *It's not cool.*

A couple of other kids appear too, and they all stand by Autumn and me. I look back at Ginger.

I...uh... she stammers. She snaps her fingers and turns around, indicating that she wants Grace and the rest of her friends to follow her. But strangely, instead of following Ginger, Grace walks up to us.

Sorry, she signs to me. I smile and shrug.

Ginger stares at Grace, but Grace doesn't budge. Ginger summons the rest of her dignity and leaves.

The group disperses and then only Autumn, Grace, and Isaac remain. They sit at the table and open their lunches as if nothing important happened. And maybe, to them, it wasn't important. But it was to me.

I finally stood up to the girl who was bullying me since sixth grade. People were being nice to me. And I made a friend. Or three. I wasn't really sure yet.

Sure, I was still deaf. And maybe I was still like Pluto. But at least Pluto has a friend.

About The Author

The signs in this story are the English translation of the real signs. There is no past tense or -ing words in ASL (American Sign Language).

Maya Bhattiprolu is a thirteen-year-old freshman. She has been writing ever since she could hold a pencil. Besides writing, she dances, reads, plays piano, and hangs out with her friends in her free time. Maya was also part of the RecycleMe group that won the Judges Choice Award in the Kid Museum Invent the Future 2018 challenge summit. She plans on joining her school newspaper when she starts high school. Maya lives with her family in Potomac, Maryland.

Deaf Like Pluto

About The Publisher

Story Shares is a nonprofit focused on supporting the millions of teens and adults who struggle with reading by creating a new shelf in the library specifically for them. The ever-growing collection features content that is compelling and culturally relevant for teens and adults, yet still readable at a range of lower reading levels.

Story Shares generates content by engaging deeply with writers, bringing together a community to create this new kind of book. With more intriguing and approachable stories to choose from, the teens and adults who have fallen behind are improving their skills and beginning to discover the joy of reading. For more information, visit storyshares.org.

Easy to Read. Hard to Put Down.

Made in the USA
Middletown, DE
20 January 2023